*This book is for my mum, Rose, and also for those
who just really appreciate a good beetle.*

Text and illustrations © 2020 Sophie Gilmore

All rights reserved. No part of this publication may be reproduced, stored in a retrieval
system, or transmitted in any form or by any means, without the prior written permission
of Owlkids Books Inc., or in the case of photocopying or other reprographic copying, a
license from the Canadian Copyright Licensing Agency (Access Copyright). For an Access
Copyright license, visit www.accesscopyright.ca or call toll-free to 1-800-893-5777.

Owlkids Books acknowledges the financial support of the Canada Council for the Arts,
the Ontario Arts Council, the Government of Canada through the Canada Book Fund
(CBF) and the Government of Ontario through the Ontario Creates Book Initiative for our
publishing activities.

Published in Canada by Owlkids Books Inc., 1 Eglinton Avenue East, Toronto, ON M4P 3A1
Published in the US by Owlkids Books Inc., 1700 Fourth Street, Berkeley, CA 94710

Library of Congress Control Number: 2019947228

Library and Archives Canada Cataloguing in Publication

Title: Freda and the blue beetle / Sophie Gilmore.
Names: Gilmore, Sophie, author, illustrator.
Identifiers: Canadiana 20190145102 | ISBN 9781771473811 (hardcover)
Classification: LCC PZ7.1.G55 F74 2020 | DDC j823/.92—dc23

Edited by Karen Li | Designed by Alisa Baldwin

Manufactured in Guangdong Province, Dongguan City, China, in October 2019,
by Toppan Leefung Packaging & Printing (Dongguan) Co., Ltd.
Job #BAYDC68

A   B   C   D   E   F

ONTARIO ARTS COUNCIL
CONSEIL DES ARTS DE L'ONTARIO
an Ontario government agency
un organisme du gouvernement de l'Ontario

Canada Council   Conseil des Arts
for the Arts   du Canada

Canadä

Publisher of Chirp, Chickadee and OWL | Owlkids Books is a division of   bayard canada
www.owlkidsbooks.com

FREDA
and the
BLUE BEETLE

by Sophie Gilmore

OWLKIDS BOOKS

FREDA didn't always listen.

"If you climb too high, you'll be swept away by the clouds," the townsfolk would warn her.

"If you swim in that bay, you'll be gulped
down by a carp," they cautioned.

Freda wasn't reckless. But she found that not listening…

often led to wonderful discoveries.

"Oh Freda," the others would sigh.

One day Freda came across a beetle with a broken wing.
"If you take that thing home, it'll bite your toes while
you sleep," the townsfolk said.

Of course, Freda didn't listen.
"Poor thing. You are safe with me."

She gave the beetle food, friendship, and a name.
They were inseparable.

In time, Ernest's shell became strong, and blue as
a winter's morning, and he grew larger every day.

The town had never known anything like Ernest. And seeing his strength, they were swift in putting him to work.

There was plenty to do.

Ernest felled trees and built their barns,

he kept watch at night,

and he toiled in their fields.

Hard work made Ernest hungry. Soon he needed more
than one folk's worth of food, though no one cared
to provide it. No matter how much Freda foraged,
it was not enough.

The townsfolk began to mutter amongst
themselves. Freda caught words like
nuisance and *brute*.

Then one terrible morning, a prize
ewe was found missing.

The mutters turned to yells. The yells grew
to bellows. Freda fought for Ernest, but it was
impossible to shut the clamor out.

Freda took Ernest to the dark forest
surrounding the town. She told Ernest sadly,
"Sometimes we have to listen."

For the town, life returned to normal, though without Ernest everyone had much more to do. The prize ewe was found, and no one would meet Freda's eyes. Eventually, all thoughts of the beetle were replaced with preparations for winter.

But for Freda, the days had lost their light.
Her heart ached for her friend, and she burned
with shame for sending him away.

Some long weeks later, a terrible storm raged. The townsfolk sheltered in the great hall as the winds grew fearsome. There was a tremendous, splintering crash—then darkness, as the roof rained down around them.

In the search for a way out, a small opening was discovered. The townsfolk took turns filling their lungs with fresh air.

When Freda's turn came, she took a measured
breath, and whispered to the wind.

As the hours ticked by, people's spirits fell.

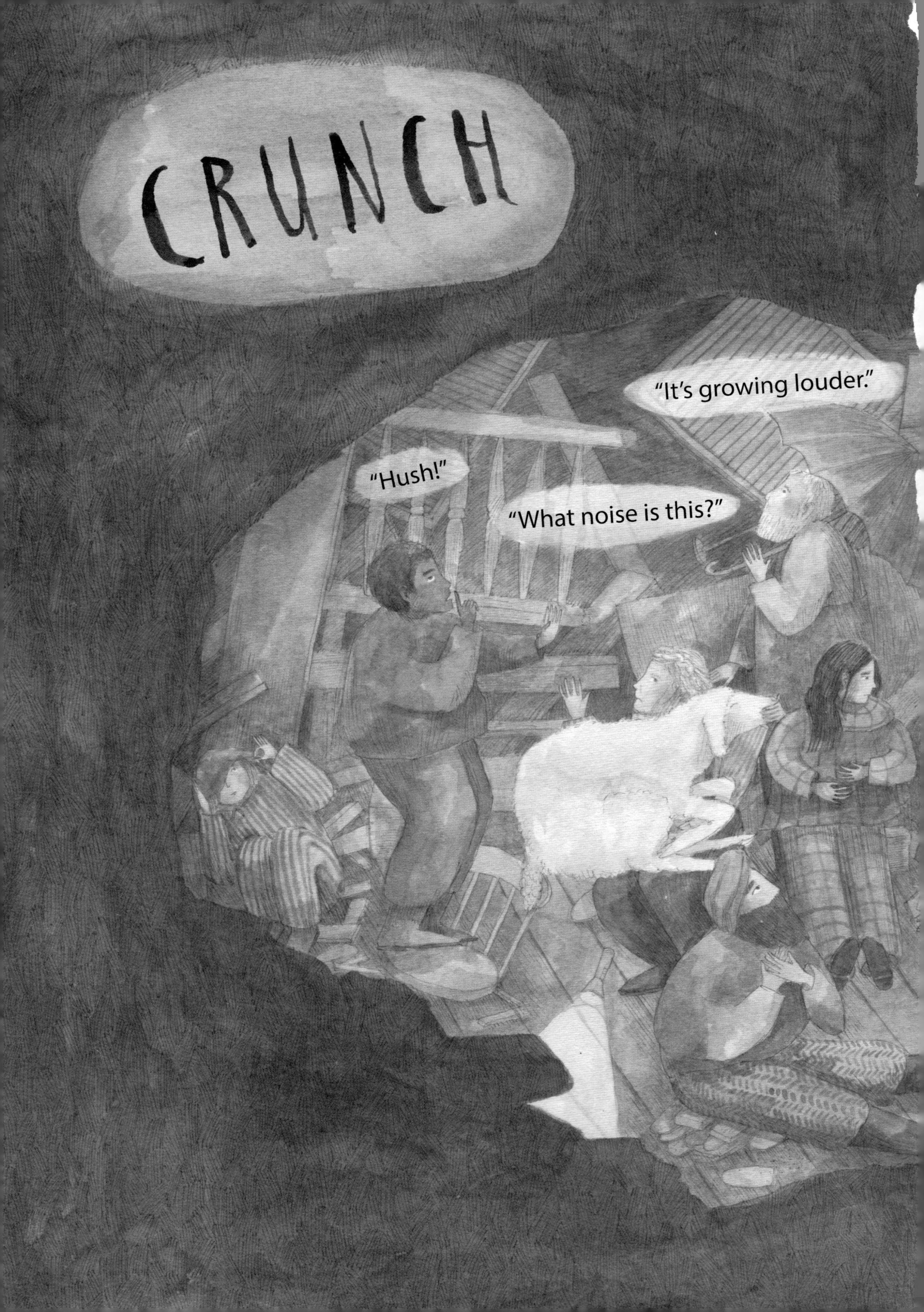
CRUNCH
"It's growing louder."
"Hush!"
"What noise is this?"

"What can you see?"
"Only the sky, blue as a winter's morning."
At these words, Freda stood.
"ERNEST."

"Ernest again, always Ernest!" the people yelled.
"The oaf will crush us with his great weight!"

Their cries rose to a clamor, joining the ever-louder
racket outside, and Freda couldn't stand the din.

But this time...

"ENOUGH,"

she hollered.
"Just listen."

And they did.

Light flooded the hollow as
Ernest ate his way through the
collapsed roof.

A chant began as the crowd climbed
out of the rubble. *"Ernest! Ernest!"*
The town rang with the sound.

But Ernest looked only at Freda,
who clambered onto his back.
She spoke quietly to her friend.

"Sometimes we should
only listen to ourselves."
Ernest fluttered his wings gently.

With Ernest before them once more, the villagers recalled just how useful he had been.

He could fell a tree like no other!

The strength of three oxen in the field!

Won't you stay, Ernest, and help us again?

"FREDA!" All eyes were now on her. "We implore you, make him see sense!"

But the wind had dropped to a breeze, the great sky beckoned…

... and Freda did not listen.